Zed Storm has lived in Japan for the past five years and is a master of several martial arts. He has a wolfhound called Max, and in his spare time plays the guitar and competes in triathlons. He likes to read about history, space exploration, and rare animals and he came up with the idea for Will Solvit while camping in a Siberian forest.

ATTENTION: ALL READERS!

Wherever you see
something that looks
like this, reach for
your decoder!
Holding it by the
corner, place
the center of
your decoder
over the lines.
Rotate it very
slowly, look
closely and,
a picture will
appear.

Mystery solved!

WILL SOLVIT

AND THE DREADED DROIDS

PaRragon

Bath · New York · Singapore · Hong Kong · Cologne · Delhi · Melbourne

Author: Zed Storm
Website: www.will-solvit.com
Creative concept and story by E. Hawken
Words by Rachel Elliot

First edition published by Parragon in 2010

Parragon
Queen Street House
4 Queen Street
Bath BA1 1HE, UK

ISBN 978-1-4075-9740-9

Printed in China

CONTENTS

Everyone knows that there are a gazillion reasons why going back to school after summer vacation isn't the best. It had been a week since my last Adventure (traveling back to ancient Egypt to fight flesh-eating mummies), and now every second I spent waiting to return to school felt like a countdown to doom.

The only exciting thing about going back was that I would be in the sixth grade. Sixth graders rule the school!

The night before school started, I went to bed with a sick feeling in the pit of my stomach. What was the point of going to school when you're an

We rule the school!

7

rrraaaarrr

Adventurer? Fighting aliens and saving the world is much more important. And finding Mom and Dad. My parents are missing, you see. The last time I saw them they were running away from a T-rex in a prehistoric jungle. In case you're wondering, I have a time machine called Morph (well, actually it's more of a machine that can turn into anything I want it to be, including a time machine), but it's broken. Or rather it has a mind of its own and won't take me anywhere I want to go—which is why I haven't rescued Mom and Dad yet.

That's another thing I should probably tell you. Since Mom and Dad went missing, I've been living with Grandpa Monty.

"Morning, Stanley," I called in through the window of the car as I jumped in the backseat.

Stanley was Grandpa Monty's driver and, as

he drove me to school that morning, he didn't say a single word the whole time. He's a little mysterious like that—I actually don't know all that much about him, other than that he's been working for Grandpa forever, and before that he used to work for the President. Can you believe it!

Anyway, that morning, Stanley dropped me off at the school gate, where my best friend, Zoe, was waiting for me. Zoe's pretty cool. She knows all about me being an Adventurer.

We headed into class, where our new teacher, Mrs. Harris, was waiting at the front of the room. We'd had Mrs. Simons last year, and she had been pretty strict, but Mrs. Harris looked a whole lot worse.

"Sit down, class!" she called at the top of her lungs. "I hope everyone is excited about being in the sixth grade."

Just the sound of Mrs. Harris's voice was sending shivers down my spine.

"Will?" Mrs. Harris's eyes narrowed as she said my name. "I trust you've brought your report on the ancient Egyptians to school—I was told you'd spent all summer working on it."

Last year I'd forgotten to write my school project on the ancient Egyptians and had to spend the entire of my summer vacation writing an extra-long report. That hadn't been as hard as I'd thought it would be, thanks to my trip back in time to ancient Egypt.

"Here you go, Mrs. Harris," I said proudly, handing her the report. "It's twenty thousand words long."

Mrs. Harris's jaw looked as though it was going to fall off and roll around the classroom.

Twenty thousand words was a lot of reading.

"Very good, Will," she said. "I'll get you to read it to the class as soon as I've made sure there are no crude jokes in there."

Then, Mrs. Harris clapped her hands before yelling out again. "OK now, class, before we get started, I need to show you all to your new lockers."

Sixth graders have the biggest lockers in the school. Zoe was given the locker next to mine.

"Isn't it weird that this time next year we'll be in a new school?" she said thoughtfully as she opened hers.

"Yeah," I nodded. "But with any luck my mom and dad will be back so I can go to a school near where I used to live…" I didn't finish what I was saying because, as I opened my locker, I could see a envelope with my name on it inside.

You see, a letter with my name on it appears whenever I go on an Adventure. I have no idea who writes them or how they always seem to know where I'm going to be, but they do.

"Zoe, look!" I whispered as I pulled the letter out. I ripped open the envelope. This is what it said...

WHAT DO YOU GET WHEN YOU CROSS A SNOWMAN WITH A VAMPIRE?
FROSTBITE.

YOU ALREADY KNOW THAT YOUR PARENTS HAVE BEEN SEPARATED AND ARE NO LONGER TOGETHER. HERE'S YOUR NEXT CLUE AS TO WHERE THEY ARE: NEITHER OF THEM IS WHERE YOU LEFT THEM. SOON YOU'LL BE TAKING A TRIP. TO FIND OUT WHERE YOU'LL BE GOING, YOU'LL NEED TO FIND A BOOK AT MONTY'S HOUSE THAT MAPS THE WORLD. TURN TO PAGE 18. YOU'LL LOVE THE RED SKIES AT NIGHT, BUT BEWARE OF THE BIRDS!

A book that mapped the world? Standing by my freshly painted locker, a thousand thoughts zoomed through my mind... If my parents weren't where I'd left them, then, where exactly had they gone? And how? Had they traveled through time? Would my new Adventure take me to them? One thing was for sure. No way would any sort of birds scare me!

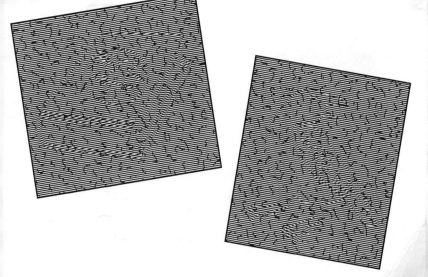

All I could think about for the rest of the day was the letter. Any Adventure that didn't lead to Mom and Dad was a waste of time as far as I was concerned. Rescuing them from wherever they had gone was more important than anything I'd ever done—even Adventures.

As the school bell rang, I bolted out of the classroom like a turbo-powered racehorse. Stanley was waiting for me in the car by the school gate, ready to drive me home. I ran toward him without looking back.

"Can I come over for dinner?" I heard Zoe shout. "I've already called my mom, and she says it's fine."

"Sure." I opened the car door and plonked myself down on the seat.

"You know, I've been thinking about the clue in your letter," she whispered to me. "A book that maps the world is clearly an atlas."

She was right, but I'd already figured that out. Zoe didn't say anything else as Stanley drove down the driveway that led to Solvit Hall before finally coming to a stop outside the front door.

Grandpa Monty was waiting for us with a big smile on his face. As we jumped out of the car, Grandpa's terrier, Plato, bolted out from behind his legs and smothered us both with big sloppy licks. Plato has to be one of the craziest dogs in the world, but he's still pretty awesome.

"So…" Grandpa winked, "how was your first day back at college?"

"I'm in sixth grade, Grandpa," I reminded him.

15

"We learned about magnetic fields in science," Zoe said enthusiastically as Stanley drove the car to the garage and we followed Grandpa into the house.

Grandpa Monty closed the front door behind him and we walked into the kitchen with Plato weaving in between my feet.

"There was a letter waiting for me in my locker today," I told him as I opened a kitchen cabinet in search of food.

"It said we needed to find a map of the world," Zoe said seriously. "Is it OK if we take a look at your atlas?"

"Of course. In the study, my dear," said Grandpa.

Quick as a flash, Zoe rushed out of the kitchen and I ran after her.

"I've been thinking," I said slowly, "I'm not

going on this Adventure, you know."

"WHAT?" Zoe swung around to face me. "What do you mean?"

"Just what I said," I went on. "Listen," I explained as I pulled her into the study and closed the door behind me—I didn't want Grandpa to hear what I was about to say. "I know I'm an Adventurer and it's my job to go on Adventures, but I've decided to sit this one out."

"But WHY?" Zoe shouted.

"Shush!!" I warned her. "I just… well… I want to spend time trying to find Mom and Dad, not going on Adventures."

"But what if the Adventure is leading you to your mom and dad?" Zoe argued as she crossed her arms over her chest. She always does that when she's annoyed.

"I don't want to risk it," I said quietly. "I've

spent all day thinking about it and I've made up my mind. You can't make me change it. Finding Mom and Dad has to be my number one priority."

Zoe stared at me long and hard. Then taking a deep breath, she launched into a huge list of reasons why I was being stupid. Like the fact that I didn't know where the Adventure would take me and that I had no idea where my parents were.

Zoe and I argued for ages… and ages… until the study door creaked open and Grandpa stuck his head around the door. "Dinner is served".

"I'm not hungry," Zoe said moodily. "I'm going to wait here until my mom picks me up, Mr. Solvit."

"Suit yourself," Grandpa said. "I'll leave a plate out for you in case you change your mind."

"Look, Zoe…" I tried to apologize as Grandpa

closed the door on us. But Zoe just turned her back on me and headed toward one of the bookshelves.

"WHATEVER!" I stormed out of the room into the kitchen, and sat down at the table. Before Grandpa could say anything, I started shoveling the food into my mouth. I was just licking my plate clean when Zoe ran into the kitchen, waving a piece of paper in her hand.

"Will, look what I've found," she said, speaking at a hundred miles an hour, "The atlas! It was in the atlas! On page eighteen! The page was ripped out, but there was an envelope with your name in its place. So I ripped it open…"

"You opened something addressed to me?" I said, starting to feel a little annoyed, to say the least.

Zoe nodded. "The letter tells you not to give

up. It says…"

"ZOE!" I shouted. I was so angry with her! "Number one, I told you I wasn't going on this Adventure. Number two, that letter was addressed to me. Number three, I don't believe you found that letter anyway. I bet you just wrote it."

Zoe looked really upset—her bottom lip had begun to quiver and she took a long breath in and out. Then she threw the letter at me and ran out of the room, slamming the door behind her.

"Something wrong with…?" Grandpa asked, but I didn't stop to talk. Quietly, I picked up the letter and ran toward my room.

Throwing the scrunched-up letter down on my bed, I lay down beside it. Then, after staring at it for a few minutes I unscrunched it and read what it said…What do Penguins have for lunch?…

WHAT DO PENGUINS HAVE FOR LUNCH? ...
ICEBERGERS.

DON'T GIVE UP, WILL. YOU'RE ABOUT TO FIND OUT
WHY THIS ADVENTURE IS SO IMPORTANT. BEING AN
ADVENTURER IS A RESPONSIBILITY, NOT A CHOICE.
HEAD FAR SOUTH, TO A TOWN BEGINNING WITH V.
VISIT DR. DEMONAX—HE'LL GIVE YOU SOME ANSWERS.

The handwriting wasn't Zoe's. It was the same
as every other letter I'd ever gotten. It had to be
authentic. But if I needed any more convincing
that my new Adventure was a waste of time, I
had it right there in front of me. There wasn't one
word about my parents in the letter.

I knew what I had to do. Feeling inside my
pocket to where Morph was in the shape of a
skating ramp (Morph always shrinks down into

a miniature version of whatever you last used it for), I programmed it to morph into a time machine. Mom and Dad might not be where I'd left them, but looking for them in the last place I'd seen them was definitely the best place to start.

I stood back as Morph spun and whirred before popping up into a time machine. I stepped inside. But there wasn't a moment to even try to enter anything into Morph's control deck. Once again, Morph wasn't taking me where I wanted to go— it was whizzing me through time to where it wanted to go. And who knew exactly where I'd end up...

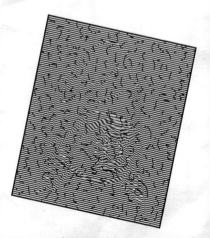

CHAPTER THREE
THE MARCHING PENGUINS

There was barely time for me to sit down, let alone throw up from the ride before Morph had stopped traveling through time and was landing with a bump. Where would I find myself when I opened the time machine door? One thing was for sure, we hadn't been traveling for very long, so we couldn't have gone very far.

Looking around me, I stupidly realized that I'd been so anxious to blast through time and find Mom and Dad that I hadn't brought any Adventurer tools. What an idiot. No stun gun, no invisibility paint, no compass that always points home—nothing.

Duh!

Nervously, I peered out of the small window in the time machine door, but I couldn't see anything much. Then the door swung open and I felt a gust of wind pump out of the time machine's air vents and push me outside. My sneakers skidded on the ground and I just about saved myself from splattering, face first, against a brick wall. I turned around, hoping to climb back into Morph, but as always, Morph had other ideas. In the blink of an eye it had shrunk back down into a miniature time machine. Typical!

"Fantastic! Just fantastic!" I said to myself. I couldn't wait for Dad to fix Morph—a time machine with a mind of its own was pretty pointless and annoying.

Slipping Morph into my pocket, I cautiously looked around. It looked as though I was standing in some kind of alleyway. There were high brick walls on either side of me, and the ground was covered with garbage. It looked like no one had cleaned up for years. "Gross," I muttered.

"Who are you?" A little voice came from behind me.

I swung around and almost didn't see the boy for a moment in the dust. He was younger than me—probably about five or six years old—and his face was covered with dirt. Not only that, he was wearing ripped and dirty pajamas.

"Aren't you a little too young to be outside without your mom and dad?" I said gently.

"I can't find them—the penguins got them," the little boy said.

Ur, rewind. Penguins? What?

"What do you mean you can't find your parents?" I asked. But the boy was now crying so hard I couldn't get another word out of him. My

How did the penguins get here???

heart softened. One thing I know a lot about is missing parents.

"I'll help you find them," I said to the boy. "Come with me." And I started to walk ahead, gesturing for the boy to follow. But he wouldn't move.

I turned around, walked back to him, and squatted on the filthy ground so I could look him in the eye. "What's your name?" I asked.

"Mikey," he sniffed.

"I'm Will. I'm trying to find my parents too," I told him.

"Were your parents also taken by the penguins?" he blubbered.

What could he be talking about?

"The penguins got everyone in my school," Mikey went on, "but I hid in the house with my mom and dad. Then we ran out of food and

Daddy had to go out to look for some, but he never came back. Then the penguins came to my house and they took my mommy. I hid under my bed, so they didn't find me. But now I'm all alone. I don't have anyone. I'm trying to find the penguins so they can take me too."

Every word coming out of Mikey's mouth sounded crazy—nothing made sense. Then I had a thought—I hadn't even tried to figure out where Morph had taken me. That might help! "Do you know what year it is?" I asked Mikey.

"It's six years after I was born and I was born in 2020," he said.

So the year was 2026. I'd traveled into the future! Cool! Although not quite so cool if the future was being run by penguins. Everything Mikey had said seemed impossible. Was he just a little boy making things up?

rikey of the alley. Suddenly a penguin appeared.
We followed the penguin and saw hundreds of people digging the ground.
Everyone looked hypnotized, with boogers coming from their noses.
There was a huge screen overlooking everyone.

There were about ten penguins staring at me, waiting for me to join the other human slaves. If I wanted to read the letter and figure out what was going on, then I had to be pretty quick…

WHAT DO YOU CALL A PENGUIN IN TIMES SQUARE…
LOST!
YOU'RE PLAYING A DANGEROUS GAME, WILL. IF YOU HAD GONE ON THE ADVENTURE YOU WERE SUPPOSED TO, THIS FUTURE WOULD NEVER HAVE HAPPENED AND HUMANKIND WOULD BE SAFE.
YOU HAVE NO CHOICE. YOU ARE AN ADVENTURER. IF YOU DO NOT DO WHAT YOU ARE MEANT TO, THEN THERE ARE CONSEQUENCES.
GET BACK TO THE TIME MACHINE. GO HOME. STOP DR. DEMONAX AND HIS ARMY.

At that moment, I felt a heavy weight push me from behind. As I toppled forward into the mud, I just about had enough time to glance over my shoulder and see a penguin looming over me. I've seen penguins before, in the zoo and on TV—but there was something weird about this one…

The penguin opened his beak as if to bite me, but instead he started speaking. "Get up. Work."

My hand brushed against my pocket to check that Morph was still sitting there. Then I stood up, turned my back on the penguin, and started walking toward the human slaves.

I knew I had only seconds to escape. But what about Mikey? I remembered what the letter had told me. I didn't have a choice.

Pulling Morph out of my pocket, I pushed my thumb onto the activation pad and threw it into the air. Morph spun and landed and then grew into a time machine. Before the penguins had a chance to stop me, I had climbed inside and was whizzing back through time.

CHAPTER FOUR
BACK TO THE PRESENT

As Morph crash-landed on my bedroom floor, I ran out of the time machine faster than you could say "Adventure". I'd seen a bunch of bizarre things since I'd become an Adventurer—angry dinosaurs, cat aliens, cursed Egyptian tombs—but a future ruled by penguins and a man with a river of snot for a nose? That had to be the weirdest!

Before Morph had a chance to shrink back down, I programmed it to turn into a computer. The only thing I could think of doing was finding out as much as I could about that man Dr. Demonax—and the Internet seemed like the best place to start.

After a few seconds, Morph had finished morphing and I quickly logged on.

Tapping the words "Dr. Demonax" into the search engine, I waited to see what came up. My eyes nearly popped like cherry-flavored bubble gum when I saw the picture on the screen...

A photo of Dr. Demonax appeared—that was definitely the man I'd seen on the screen. Only there was someone with him in the photo, and they were shaking hands. As I looked more closely I started to tremble. It was the hand of someone I knew pretty well—it was my dad's hand! And underneath the picture was a caption:

Henry Solvit and Dr. Demonax: the world's two greatest inventors ever.

My brain whirred into overdrive. Dr. Demonax was an inventor, just like my dad? And my dad had shaken the hand of the man who would one day enslave humankind? How could this be?

I spent hours looking on the Internet but couldn't find any other information about Dr. Demonax. Feeling desperate, the next best thing I could think of was asking another Adventurer— Grandpa Monty.

Running down the stairs, I went to find him as quickly as possible.

"Grandpa?"

"Yes?"

"Did Dad ever tell you much about Dr. Demonax?"

Grandpa banged his fist on the kitchen table. "How do you know that name?" he bellowed.

With my mouth gaping as wide as a basketball court, I stuttered, "Um... uh..."

"No matter what anyone says, you must never speak that name again, do you understand?"

OOPS!

Grandpa's eyes looked like lightning was bouncing around inside of them. I'd never seen him look so mad. "You do not speak of that man, you do not try to find out about him, and you certainly never try to find him. No Adventure should take you to him."

"Yes, Grandpa," I said a little shakily. But before I had the chance to ask any more, the phone started to ring.

Stanley appeared in the doorway, holding the receiver in his hand. "It's for you, Will," he said.

"It's me, Zoe," said the voice at the other end.

I walked away from the kitchen, into Grandpa's study, shutting the door behind me before I said anything. "Something mega-weird is going on," I started. "Lots has happened since I last saw you..."

I told her about traveling into the future, about

Mikey, the penguins, and everyone being snotty slaves. "So I looked up Dr. Demonax on the Internet," I went on. "And it turns out that he's an inventor my dad knew. But when I asked Grandpa about him he totally flipped out." I paused for Zoe to speak, but she stayed silent. "I'm sorry I yelled at you," I finished.

"So you believe I didn't write the letter now?"

"Of course," I answered.

"Listen, Will," she said seriously. "After I left your house I did some some research into Dr. Demonax myself. He went to college with your dad—they used to work on inventions together. Apparently Dr. Demonax helped your dad do experiments with dark energy."

Dark energy! "Like Morph," I said quickly. "Morph uses dark energy to power itself. If Dr. Demonax knows about dark energy, then he must

I have to find him!

know about Morph!"

"Yup," said Zoe. I could imagine her grinning from ear to ear as she spoke into the phone. "If anyone will know how to fix Morph's time machine program, he will. He could be the key to helping you find your parents!"

There were no two ways about it. I had to find Dr. Demonax—to stop him from taking over the world with his penguin army, but also to get him to fix Morph. But how are you supposed to get a scientist to help you with something? Especially one who was potentially evil?

"Look out of the study window," Zoe said.

Quickly, I walked across the room and saw Zoe outside in the yard. She was wearing a winter coat, wool hat, gloves, snow boots, and a thick scarf.

"Where do you think you're going?" I laughed.

"Skiing in the Arctic?"

"No," beamed Zoe, walking toward the window. "The Antarctic—and you're coming with me."

I hung up the phone and shouted through the window, "What are you talking about?"

Zoe pointed to the catch on the window, so I pushed it back and swung it open. Zoe pulled herself up before scrambling through the window.

"Isn't it obvious where we have to go?" she said, taking her coat off and trying to cool herself down.

"Ur, no?" I said, puzzled. "Not exactly."

"The clue was in the first letter," Zoe said. "Red sky at night..."

I stared at her blankly—I had no idea what she was going on about.

"The aurora australis?" she went on.

"The whata what?" I raised my eyebrow.

"The southern lights, Will," Zoe explained, rolling her eyes. "You see the northern lights at the North Pole and the southern lights at the South Pole."

"I have no idea what you're talking about," I said.

"Uh…never mind," she said, frustrated. "But listen, when the second letter came, it said you had to go as far south as you could, which obviously means the South Pole. So I looked at an atlas back at home—one that didn't have pages ripped out of it—and sure enough, there's a town beginning with V, like the letter said, called Vostok—it's the closest you can get to the south pole."

"And you think this is where Dr. Demonax will be?" I asked.

Zoe grinned like a demented baboon and nodded. "Three guesses what kinds of birds live at the South Pole."

I didn't need three guesses—Penguins!

A smile crept over my face in a split second. "Well, what are we waiting for? We need to figure out a plan."

"Already did it," she smiled as she pushed a neatly folded piece of paper into my hands. I unfolded it, and this is what it said.

Zoe and Will's Antarctic Adventure
Plan of Action:

1) Pack warm clothes
2) Travel to the ocean
3) Turn Morph into a submarine
4) Travel underwater to Antarctica

5) Turn Morph into a snowmobile so we can travel across Antarctica
6) Cross Antarctica to Vostok
7) Speak to Dr. Demonax
8) Fix Morph
9) Rescue Will's Mom and Dad
10) Come back in time for school tomorrow

"I'm impressed," I said to her.

Zoe grinned.

"Two things you got wrong, though..."

"What?" Her smile quickly vanished from her face as I began to speak.

"First, we need to find out how and why Dr. Demonax got so mental and try to stop him. And second, there's no way we'll make it back in time for school tomorrow. Still, there's not much we can do about that," I said, folding the note up and passing it back to her. And before Zoe had a chance to argue with me, I turned and walked out of the room.

"Where are you going, Will?"

"I need to write a note of my own before I, or rather we, go anywhere," I said to her.

Pulling a pad and pen out of my backpack, I began to write.

Dear Grandpa Monty,

I've run away to the South Pole to stop Dr. Demonax from taking over the world. I've taken Morph Zoe and my winter coat. Be home as soon as possible.

Love,

Will

I'm getting mega quick at packing for an Adventure. This is what I packed in about two seconds flat:

- Morph
- Winter coat
- Gloves, hat, and scarf
- Grandpa's spy journal
- Compass that always points home

Zoe and I tiptoed down the stairs as quietly as two mice with slippers on—there was no way I wanted Grandpa to see me running away. He'd put a stop to it, for sure.

We made it down the stairs and toward the front door without making a sound. Just as I put my hand on the doorknob, Plato came running towards us yapping his fluffy head off.

"Shush!" I whispered, begging him to shut up. But he only yapped louder, as if he wanted to warn Grandpa.

"What's going on out there?" Grandpa shouted from the kitchen.

"We need to get out of here, fast!" Zoe whispered through gritted teeth. "If Monty finds out what we're up to we're busted!"

Plato yapped louder and louder and started growling at me, biting on my trouser leg and pulling me towards the kitchen. "Not now, mate," I pleaded with him, "shush!"

"Will, is that you?" Grandpa called, sounding worried.

"Just me, Monty," said a voice out of nowhere—Stanley. "You sit back down, I was just about to drive home for the night. Plato seems to want me to stay."

"Very well," I heard Grandpa mutter.

Stanley walked down the hall toward us. He winked at me and reached for the front door. Zoe and I quickly tiptoed out of the house. Stanley followed us and closed the heavy front door behind him—making sure yappy Plato stayed inside.

"What you up to, Will?" Stanley asked with a suspicious glint in his eye.

"Official Adventurer business," I replied, still whispering. "But Grandpa can't know, not yet."

Stanley eyed me doubtfully before saying, "So I guess you'll want a ride somewhere?"

"To the coast actually," Zoe said before I could

Totally
cool guy!

come up with something clever to throw Stanley off the scent.

"Well let's go then—it'll be dark soon," Stanley said.

I wasn't sure if letting Stanley drive us to the coast was the best move, but it seemed to be the only choice I had.

We all climbed in the car and Stanley drove us down the driveway of Solvit Hall. We drove all the way to the coast in silence. Stanley didn't ask what we were up to and Zoe and I weren't giving anything away. It took three and a half hours to get to the sea and it was pitch black by the time we got there.

"I'll drop you off by the pier," Stanley said to us.

The car pulled up by the pier and Zoe climbed out, I leant towards Stanley, "Will you give this to Grandpa Monty please?" I passed him the note I'd written to Grandpa. "Tell him not to worry about me, I'll be fine."

"Sure thing, Will," Stanley smiled as I got out the car.

Stanley drove off and Zoe and I walked down the pier. The wooded planks of the pier creaked beneath our feet and I could hear the ocean's waves crash over the rocks below. The sea was lit by a full moon.

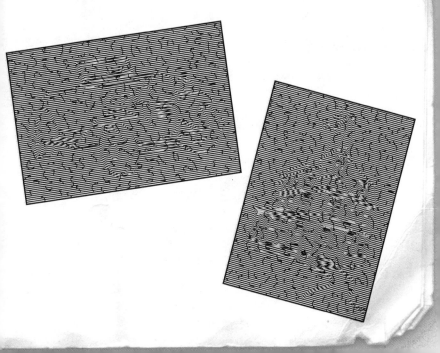

I took Morph out of my pocket and activated it.

Then I typed in "Submarine," and dropped Morph into the water.

Morph splashed around and turned into a submarine. The top popped open.

Zoe and I climbed down the ladder. The submarine began to sink into the ocean.

Down below we found a control deck to program coordinates.

"I don't suppose you know the coordinates of where we're going?" I asked Zoe, hoping against hope that she did.

Zoe, being Zoe, pulled a piece of paper out of her bag and handed it to me. Score!

I tapped the coordinates into the control panel before pressing the green button for go. Morph started to move through the gloomy waters, crawling slowly through the murky ocean. Gradually, however, we picked up speed, and soon Morph was traveling as fast as any Nascar! Just when I thought we couldn't go any faster, Morph started to zoom through the water even more quickly, going deeper as well. Soon we were hurtling through the ocean faster than a plane.

"This is so amazing," Zoe said wistfully, gazing out of the porthole. Then suddenly she

Aaarrghh!
Scary!

screamed, jumping backwards as the face of a shark appeared inches from the window.

The shark seemed to be fascinated by Morph and swam alongside us forever before it finally got bored, flicked its tail, and swam off.

In no time at all, Morph was traveling so fast that we couldn't see anything out of the portholes other than rushing water. Zoe and I sat down. She got out her notebook and started writing, and I got out Grandpa Monty's spy journal and started to read.

It was good, because it gave me something to think about besides the horrible future I'd be traveling to in order to stop Dr. Demonax from turning Mikey's parents, and every other human, into snot-faced slaves. It only took me a few pages of diary reading to realize that Grandpa Monty had been to the Antarctic too...

Yuk!

July 14, 1956

If you're scared of snakes, pack up your thermal underwear and move to Antarctica. It's the only continent with no reptiles at all!

The Antarctic is an amazing place, full of incredible wildlife, and the red sky at night is nothing short of spectacular. I've been staying at the Vostok research center for a month now; we haven't learned anything new about the Partek.

However, there are some fascinating things about the Antarctic. For starters, the South Pole was first reached in 1911. Not only that, but over 98% of Antarctica is covered by ice. Animals living there include the penguin, seals, and birds, and it's the windiest place on earth—fact! There are no countries in Antarctica, only ice.

Will write again soon

Mont

I fell asleep with Grandpa's diary in my hands. About twelve hours later I woke up to Zoe shaking me and shouting in my ear, "Wake up, Will. We're here!"

Grandpa's diary fell to the floor as I jumped to my feet and rushed toward the nearest window. There was no murky water outside anymore. Instead there was bright white ice. Quickly, I pulled on my coat and climbed the ladder leading to the hatch at the top of the submarine. As I pushed the hatch open, a sea of light flooded my eyes. When my eyes finally adjusted, I could see the deep blue ocean behind us, bobbing with gentle waves, whereas ahead of us there was nothing but ice and snow—the Antarctic. Zoe was right. We had arrived.

"I looked around the submarine when you were sleeping," Zoe said, climbing back down the ladder and pointing to a door that sat slightly open. Walking over, I looked inside to find everything anyone could possibly ever need for a South Pole expedition: snowsuits, skis, sleds. Among all the gear was an envelope with my name on it.

Quickly, I read my letter.

WHY DO PENGUINS CARRY FISH IN THEIR BEAKS? . . . BECAUSE THEY DON'T HAVE ANY POCKETS.

TAKE EVERYTHING YOU NEED FROM MORPH. WHEN YOU FIND DR. DEMONAX, YOU CAN'T LET HIM KNOW WHY YOU'RE HERE. MAKE HIM TRUST YOU—ONLY THEN WILL YOU DISCOVER HOW TO STOP HIM...

CUT THEM OFF AT THE SOURCE.

I had no idea what "cut them off at the source" meant. I really wished that whoever wrote these letters didn't always have to be so cryptic!

I handed Zoe the letter, and as she read it, I zipped myself into a snowsuit.

Struggling to get everything we needed out of Morph and onto the ice outside, we were finally ready. I quickly deactivated Morph, shrinking it back down to a mini-submarine before slipping it into my bag.

I looked at Zoe and gave her a smile. "Ready for an Adventure?"

"You bet."

Then, before I had a chance to say anything else, she was lowering her ski goggles, climbing onto her skis, and skidding over the snow. Taking a deep breath, I followed her, and we slipped and slid over the ice until finally we came to an edge with a big drop below. I took a big gulp. I'd been skiing before, but never on anything as steep as this. Zoe was clearly a pro, and she swept off down the slope. Taking another deep breath, I followed her, and before I knew it, we were at the bottom. In front of us lay a sheet of ice.

"We'll have to turn Morph into a snowmobile," I said.

"Good idea," said Zoe.

Quick as a flash, I activated the keyboard, and a red snowmobile sprang up in front of us.

I climbed aboard and Zoe jumped on behind. I fired up the ignition and we were off, speeding and sliding across the ice.

And there was worse to come… Ice picks came in handy when we climbed up a sheer rock face.

We bungee jumped down a canyon.

As we landed we passed a flock of penguins, who immediately began to follow us.

"Since when have penguins been so interested in humans?" asked Zoe.

We took a moment to stop for a rest which was a big mistake. No sooner had we stopped than the penguins began to attack us. They opened their beaks and pecked at us, ripping our snowsuits.

"Stop!" I cried.

We fought bravely. Then, just as I thought we were done for, a snowmobile appeared on the horizon. My heart missed a beat as it headed toward us. The snowmobile wasn't your usual snowmobile—this one was being pulled by a fleet of penguins. But even so, it wasn't that that had made my heart go into overdrive. It wasn't that at all. What had panicked me wasn't the animals in charge of the vehicle but the figure I could see at the wheel. As the snowmobile got closer and closer, I could see that the driver was none other than Dr. Demonax. And there was nowhere for us to hide!

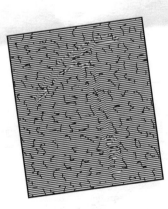
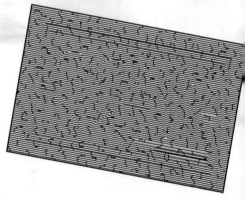

"I'm Dr. Demonax, hop on board," a voice boomed.

The snowmobile didn't even stop to pick us up—we just had to jump on as it was zooming past. We had no choice. The penguins would have killed us for sure.

"Out of the way, you beastly birds! Ha ha!" Dr. Demonax cackled loudly as he steered his snowmobile through the crowds of crazed penguins. "I've been expecting you," he grinned at me as we raced away.

"What is up with those penguins?" I shouted, amazed that I was actually alive and not bird food.

"Perfectly normal behavior for Antarctic penguins," Dr. Demonax replied, turning away from me and steering the penguins pulling the snowmobile. I knew he was lying. There was no way it was normal for penguins to attack humans, just like it wasn't normal for them to act like prison guards or open their beaks to speak! By the look of things, every penguin in the Antarctic was just as bad as the ones in the future—but why?

My eyes stared into the side of Dr. Demonax's face as he drove through the snow. He looked pretty normal, although he did have an abnormal amount of snotty green icicles poking out the end of his nose. Looking at him, knowing he'd cause so much pain and torture in the future, I really wanted to just throw him off the snowmobile and let him get eaten by the penguins. But the letter had told me to make Dr. Demonax trust me, so throwing him to certain death-by-penguin wasn't really an option.

Zoe shot me a worried look before she wrinkled her nose as she spoke to Dr. Demonax.

"So why do you live out here?" she asked.

Dr. Demonax turned to her. "And just who are you?" he asked. "I'd recognize Will Solvit anywhere—he looks just like his dad—but you…"

"I'm Zoe," she said, sounding annoyed. "I'm Will's friend. Where are you taking us?"

"Back to my laboratory. It's the only place you'll be able to get warm and have a hot meal."

Dr. Demonax said every word slowly and carefully, like an actor on a stage.

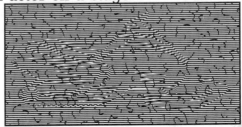

Dr. Demonax reminded me a little of my dad. Although he looked like a crazy scientist.

We rode on the snowmobile for what seemed like hours.

Something looked really strange about the penguins but I couldn't work out what it was.

The penguins' eyes spun in their heads like spinning tops.

Zoe leaned over and whispered to me, "Are they like the penguins in the future?" She spoke so quietly, only I could hear her.

I nodded. "They look kind of weird, don't they?"

"Robotic if you ask me," she said.

Robotic?! Zoe was right. I should have figured it out sooner. The penguins were robots—that would certainly explain why they were able to speak! But there wasn't time to dwell on it now— we were pulling up to a large dome-shaped building with a chimney, although there was no smoke coming out of it, which surprised me, given how cold it was.

"We're here!" Dr. Demonax shouted. "My laboratory—at the bottom of the world. Ha ha!"

WILL'S
FACT FILE

Dear Adventurer,

Not so long ago, people didn't have computers, cell phones, and MP3 players. So who knows what will be invented next?

Pushing the boundaries of science and technology is one of the greatest adventures imaginable, and there are hundreds of cool things still waiting to be invented—maybe you could be the one to invent them!

Luckily for you, this amazing fact file will put you well on your way to being a high-tech know-it-all Adventurer!

WHAT IS A ROBOT?

You've probably heard the word "robot" used countless times. But have you ever considered exactly what robots are?

A droid is another name for robot.

A robot is composed entirely, or almost entirely, from artificial substances.

A robot can sense its environment, and manipulate or interact with things in it.

A robot is programmed to be able to make choices based on its environment.

Robots are programmable.

A robot is a machine that can complete a series of actions automatically.

Robots can move and rotate.

Robots can be any shape or size.

Robots move without direct human intervention.

The study, design, and manufacturing of robots is called Robotics.

Robots are built with specific purposes.

Electronic circuits make robots move. These can be controlled by radio signal or a computer.

The word "robot" comes from the Czech word for work or labor.

Robots cannot feel emotions. However, they can be built to have senses.

Television cameras are a type of robot and have light-sensitive cells that help them "see."

A Walker Robot is a robot that moves on legs rather than wheels or tracks.

A Hexapod Robot is the name of a robot that walks on six legs.

Some robots have touch-sensitive pads that enable them to pick up delicate objects without breaking them.

Virtual Reality is a series of effects produced by a computer that enables someone wearing special equipment to feel as if they are really within an artificially created world.

An android is a robot shaped like a human being.

A Cartesian Robot is a robot whose movements can only happen at right angles to one another.

Animatronics is a method of animating models by using specially developed robotic techniques.

An Articulated Robot is a robot that has rotating joints.

Elektro was the world's first humanoid robot, and was built by Westinghouse in 1939.

Elektro was seven feet tall and "spoke" more than 700 words.

Leonardo da Vinci drew up plans for an armored humanoid machine in 1495.

Some robots are programmed to learn from their mistakes and not repeat them.

A Bipedal Robot is a robot that walks on two legs.

Cybernetics professor Kevin Warwick calls himself the world's first cyborg, with computer chips implanted in his left arm. He can remotely operate doors, an artificial hand, and an electronic wheelchair.

A Robosapien is a toylike, pet robot.

History's first robot can be traced all the way back to the ancient Greeks—a guy called Archytas of Tarentum built a mechanical bird driven by a jet of steam or compressed air.

· In the 1940s Isaac Asimov wrote the Three Laws of Robotics:
1. A robot may not injure a human or allow a human being to come to harm
2. A robot must obey the orders give by humans, except where such order would conflict with the First Law.
3. A robot must protect its own existence, as long as such protectio does not conflict with the First or Second Law.

Asimov's law

· Japan is the robot capital of the world.
· It is home to 30 percent of all the world's robots.
· The Japanese even have a robotic shopping cart.
· Did you know? A single robot is said to be able to do the work of 10 Japanese factory workers.

Japan—robot capital of the world!

· Robots are great at performing boring jobs around the clock.
· Some industrial robots are enormous. Skywash is a giant robo arm that cleans jumbo jets.
· Did you know? Robots can go wrong. In 1988 robots in a Michigan car factory went berserk—smashing windows a painting one another.

Skywash

Robots are used to deactivate booby-trapped bombs, handle dangerous chemicals, and explore dangerous areas of the Earth, such as volcanos.
Robot security guards patrol some high-tech homes and offices.
BEAR (Battle Extraction Assist Robot) is designed to rescue injured people from a battlefield or collapsed building.

BEAR

· Jason Junior, or JJ, is an underwater robot that can withstand high pressures that would crush a human.
· JJ can be launched and controlled from a mother ship on the surface.
· JJ can dive to depths of 200,000 feet.
· In 1986 Jason Junior was used to explore the wreck of the Titanic.

Jason Junior

·With robot-assisted surgery, surgeons don't have to be present.
· Robo-docs are mobile robots that allow patients to communicate with a doctor via the video screen they have.
· In the future, robots might be small enough to enter your bloodstream. These nanorobots might be able to diagnose, investigate, and treat disease.

Robo-doc

- Since they were first introduced in 1963, flexible robotic arms have been helping amputees lead a normal life.
- Hal is a robotic suit that people can wear to improve their physical capabilities.
- Did you know? The 1970s TV character the Six Million Dollar Man had superhuman strength thanks to many robotic parts.

Robotic hand!

- Since the 1960s unmanned robotic spacecraft have been exploring parts of space where no human would survive.
- A space probe is a robot that orbits a planet picking up information.
- Rovers travel across planet surfaces, gathering information and samples.
- In 1997 Sojourner Rover became the first robot to travel across another planet.

Sojourner Rover

- Dextre is a two-armed robot used to service the International Space Station.
- It was sent into space in March 2008.
- Dextre is equipped with two 10-foot-long arms.
- It can remove and replace small parts on the space station's exterior.

DEXTRE

Maria, the evil villain in the 1927 film Metropolis, was the first android to star in a movie.

CP3O and R2D2 are the comical robotic stars in the Star Wars movies.

Lt. Commander Data is the almost human android in Star Trek: The Next Generation.

Robots is a 2005 computer-generated film starring a robot called Rodney Copperbottom.

Maria

· Robosaurus is a huge fire-breathing dinosaur robot.
· It uses hydraulics to lift and destroy cars, trucks and planes.
· It is over 40 feet high.
· It is controlled by a driver who sits in its head.
· It is a transformer and can even transform into its own trailer for transportation.

Robosaurus

· Robots are slowly working their way into our homes.
· When RB5X hit the stores in 1985, it became the first robot kit that anyone could buy.
· PaPeRo are tiny personal robots that can speak over 3,000 words, tell the time, and dance!
· Robosapien is an affordable entertainment robot that comes to life at your command.

PaPeRo

- ASIMO is a two-legged robot that can walk upright and climb stairs.
- Actroid is a female robot that looks like a Japanese woman and mimics human behavior.
- Manny is a humanoid robot used to test firefighting clothing!

ASIMO

- Kismet is a disembodied robotic head that can change its facial expressions to show fear, joy, and surprise.
- Kismet changes its expression by moving its ears, eyebrows, eyelids, lips, jaw, and head.
- It is designed to interact with and respond to humans.

KISMET

- The more legs a robot has the better it moves around, so animal robots are normally pretty agile.
- AIBO is a robotic dog that can recognize 75 different words and comes when it's called.
- Para is a seal robot companion that can open and close its eyes and move its flippers.

AIBO

The sky was really dark now with amazing ribbons of bright clouds that shimmered like stars. I'd never seen anything as cool as the bands of color that moved and squirmed across the sky.

"The aurora australis," Zoe smiled at me. "The southern lights."

But now that we had stopped moving, something pretty weird seemed to be happening to the penguins. It was almost as if they were shutting down, the way a machine does. As if someone had flicked an "off" switch in their brain. If I needed any more proof that the penguins were robots—that was it.

Zoe reached out to touch one of the penguins as we climbed off the snowmobile.

"No touching my pets!" Dr. Demonax shouted at her. "I wouldn't want you to get bitten.

He is TOTALLY nuts!

Penguin bites sting like wasps—ha ha ha!"

"Ur, OK." I raised my eyebrow. Dr. Demonax wasn't just an evil inventor—he was weird with a capital W!

Taking a deep breath, I followed as Dr. Demonax led us inside the laboratory. It looked like a giant greenhouse now that we were up close. The whole thing was made of glass, and through the roof you could see the southern lights in the sky. A huge pillar stood in the middle of the lab, running from the floor to the ceiling, which I guessed was probably connected to the chimney I'd seen on the outside of the lab—only up close it didn't look like a chimney at all. It just looked like a large pillar of black glass.

"You two make yourselves at home," he said to us with a twisted grin. "I've got a few things to take care of."

And, without another word, Dr. Demonax walked back outside into the cold.

As soon as we had thawed out, Zoe and I took our snowsuits off and walked around in our normal clothes—my bones were frozen through.

"Let's look around," I said to Zoe. "If Dr. Demonax's penguins are robots, like we think they are, there must be a way to stop them from working."

Zoe looked thoughtful. "Didn't your letter say something about cutting them off at the source?"

Genius! "That's it!" I smiled. "We have to find the source of the robots' power and somehow cut it off."

We spent ages walking around Dr. Demonax's large, glass laboratory. It was full of crazy things, but nothing that looked like a droid army power supply. We wandered over to the glass sides of the lab to look out onto the red night sky.

"I wonder if people back home are worried about us," Zoe said quietly.

"I wonder..." I started, but I didn't have a chance to finish my sentence because Zoe started screaming. I covered my ears at the sound, then nearly jumped out of my skin when I saw what she was screaming at.

Dr. Demonax was standing outside, gazing in at us. He looked terrifying. His whole face and body were covered with a strange plastic suit. Without saying anything, he reached his plastic-covered hand toward us. But his hand didn't stop moving when it hit the glass. Instead, the glass started to ripple like the surface of a pond when you throw a stone in. Slowly, his fingers moved through the glass toward us. Then came his hand, his arm, his chest, his face, and his legs.

Scary, but AWESOME!

Before we knew it, Dr. Demonax was standing in front of us, inside the glass dome, and smiling his stomach-flipping grin.

"Do you like my suit?" he asked, peeling the plastic from his face. "One of my new inventions. It can move through glass—clever, isn't it? Your father never invented anything like this, Will, did he?" he said smugly, as a globule of snot from his nose hit the floor with a splash.

"No, not that I know of," I said, hiding a look of disgust.

"So, Will," Dr. Demonax said, peeling the rest of the plastic suit from his clothes, "why are you here? Did Henry send you to spy on me? Ha ha ha."

Zoe and I flinched at the sound of his voice.

"No," I stuttered, realizing that I had no idea what to tell him. "I'm here because... because..."

My brain scrambled overtime to find a good excuse. "Because Mom and Dad have gone missing and I need you to help me find them," I blurted out.

"Missing?" he said, surprised.

"That's why I'm here," I said cautiously. "I need you to help me find my parents."

"I couldn't possibly do that, Will," Dr. Demonax said, walking away from me and shaking his head. "To even start looking for Henry I'd need a Morphing Anatomical Dark Energy Device, and there's only one of those in existence. Your dad—"

"I have it here," I said, cutting him off quickly as I dug my hand into my bag and pulled out Morph. "I used Morph as a submarine and snowmobile to get to you—"

Before I had a chance to finish my sentence,

Dr. Demonax had whipped Morph out of my
hands and was cradling it in his palms like a
precious stone. His eyes were wide, wild, and
crazed as he stroked Morph like a pet hamster
and whispered something to himself.

Zoe and I walked toward him and listened to
what he was saying.

"At last… it's mine… the Morphing Anatomical
Dark Energy Device is mine… at last."

Do dinosaur farts stink? How stupid had I been
handing Morph over to Dr. Demonax. For a split
second I had forgotten that Dr. Demonax was
evil. How could I even have thought that handing
Morph over to him would be a good idea?

Zoe looked at me as if she wanted to jump

down my throat and start knitting a sweater with my intestines—she was M-A-D!

"I have to make him trust me," I whispered feebly to her.

"How could it help to give our only chance of escape to an evil scientist who's planning to take over the world?" she asked furiously.

I shrugged. I knew she was right. What had I done? But my only choice was to make Dr. Demonax trust me, wasn't it? And Dr. Demonax was the only person, other than Dad, who had a hope of fixing Morph.

Three entire days passed. No new letters, no clues, no leads, no hope. We ate cold canned food for every meal and slept on the cold, hard

TOTALLY gross!

floor in sleeping bags every night. Dr. Demonax never went to sleep. Instead, he spent every minute of every day playing with Morph—he turned it into a race car, a radio, an MP3 player, a speedboat, even a helicopter. Every time I tried to speak to him he would give me the same answer: "Not yet—I haven't figured out how it works."

Of course I was pretty worried about finding a way to stop Dr. Demonax from taking over the world. But his obsession with Morph was buying us time to explore the laboratory.

While Dr. Demonax spent his days fiddling with Morph and shouting at it every time it did something he didn't understand, Zoe and I used the time to explore. We chased the droid penguins—didn't manage to catch one. We studied the crazy inventions in the lab. We told each other jokes, dug in the snow—only found more snow, and had snowball fights.

Every single day Dr. Demonax tried to ask me questions about Dad while he was prodding Morph with a screwdriver. I avoided answering them as much as possible. I still had no clue how to stop him from taking over the world, and he had no clue how to fix Morph.

"Will, we've been here for a whole week," Zoe said with concern, as we walked through the thick snow surrounding the lab. "What about school? What about my mom? I bet she's really, really worried. I know the letter said to make Dr. Demonax trust you, but that doesn't seem to be getting us anywhere. Maybe we should just try asking him."

"Try asking him what, exactly? Excuse me, Dr. Demonax, is your brain made of boogers? Is your

Booger brain

brain running out of your nose? Is that why you think taking over the world is a good idea? Do you fuel your droids with snot dribbles?"

"Look, I don't see you coming up with any better ideas," said Zoe.

"No," I shouted. "Maybe I haven't, but..."

My eyes lit up as I noticed an envelope with my name on it sitting in the snow.

"Quick, Will, open it," Zoe said, spotting the letter too.

WHAT DID THE TISSUE SAY TO THE NOSE? ...
DON'T GET SNOTTY WITH ME!

YOU'VE DONE WELL SO FAR, WILL. GIVING MORPH TO
DR. DEMONAX MAY HAVE FELT STUPID, BUT YOU DID
THE RIGHT THING.
BUT NOW YOU MUST STOP DR. DEMONAX. FIND THE
SOURCE OF HIS POWER... CUT THE DROIDS OFF AT THE
SOURCE... YOU MUST FOIL HIS EVIL PLANS—IF YOU
DON'T, THE WHOLE WORLD WILL BE IN DANGER.

Zoe read the letter over my shoulder.

"Oh no!" she said.

"Oh yes!" said a voice behind us. Zoe wasn't the only one reading the letter over my shoulder—Dr. Demonax was too! He ripped it out of my hands, blowing a snot bubble of rage.

"Who wrote this letter?" he demanded.

"Why should I tell you?" I said angrily. "We know what you're planning and we're going to take you down!"

Dr. Demonax let out one of his crazy, cackling laughs. "Ha ha ha, stupid child! You think you can stop me?"

He grabbed Zoe's and my arms and twisted them until we both cried out in pain. He whistled really loudly and two penguins appeared out of nowhere. As we struggled to break free of Dr. Demonax's clutches, the penguins came and grabbed the sleeves of our snowsuits in their beaks before pulling us towards the entrance of the laboratory.

"Lock them in the basement!" Dr. Demonax shouted to the penguins.

I heard Dr. Demonax cackling behind me as another penguin ran past us and started jumping up and down on the floor. Suddenly a trap door sprang open and a huge hole appeared in the ground.

My feet stopped still. I knew what was coming, and I wanted to stop it. Zoe was thrown into the hole first. I heard her scream as she fell downward and hit the ground below with a thud.

The penguins gave me a push, and I felt myself fall down and down and down...

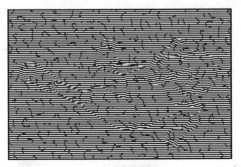

CHAPTER SEVEN
PENGUIN POWER

So Zoe and I were in Antarctica, locked in the basement of a secret laboratory, and the only person who knew we were there was an evil scientist who was plotting to take over the world with the help of an army of droid penguins. I was starting to panic when a light switch clicked and the dark room flooded with light.

"Will, look!" I heard Zoe scream as my eyes adjusted to the light.

We were standing in a small dungeon, a room not much bigger than a closet. It reminded me of my dad's laboratory back home—the walls were covered with crowded shelves.

How dumb?

Dr. Demonax was the stupidest smart person I'd ever met—he'd just locked us in a room full of inventions, inventions that just might help us escape. As I looked around the room my eyes took in a few familiar objects—invisibility paint, walkie-talkie earplugs, a periscope, a pair of goggles, and a freeze gun.

"Quick, grab as much stuff as you can," I said to Zoe as I ran toward the nearest shelf and started loading my pockets with useful inventions.

Picking up the pair of goggles sitting on the shelf, I went to put them on when I spotted a small scrap of paper inside them with the same handwriting as my letters.

WILL, TAKE THESE GOGGLES— THEY'LL HELP YOU SEE THINGS THAT OTHER PEOPLE CAN'T.

There wasn't time to figure out what the note meant, but the goggles must be important. I put them on quickly, but everything looked normal. I'd have to figure out why they were special later. There was an empty canvas backpack lying on the floor, so I picked it up and stuffed the inventions into it.

Zoe and I were so busy going through Dr. Demonax's inventions that it took us a while to realize there was a small door between the shelves. Zoe reached for the handle and turned it, but it was locked. Pulling out the amulet that I always wear around my neck, I wondered if it would act as a key. I had found the amulet in one of the first letters that I received, and not only did it help me speak other languages, but it could open locks. Only it looked as though it wasn't going to work this time. The lock needed a regular key. We looked around, but there was nothing in sight.

"I might be able to pick the lock," Zoe said shyly.

"What?" I said, amazed. "Since when can you pick locks?"

"It's not a skill I'm proud of," she said defensively. "My dad taught me how to do it, in case I ever got locked in somewhere I needed to get out of."

"Like now," I said, stepping back from the door so she could have a stab at it.

I watched silently as Zoe pulled a bobby pin from her hair, unbent it, and started poking the lock. As she bit her lip in concentration, she twiddled the bobby pin around until suddenly there was a clicking sound—the lock had opened!

"Nice one, Zoe," I cried.

Slowly, I pulled the door open. It was mega-stiff but I had it and soon an enormous gust of freezing cold air was blasting in on us and hitting us like a gale.

"Brrr," I shivered.

Behind the door was a corridor carved out of ice. It sparkled like sunlight on snow and felt like stepping into a giant freezer.

"I wonder what's at the end of the corridor," I muttered. "Only one way to find out." I took a step into the corridor.

"Wait!" Zoe said nervously. "Don't you think we should split up?"

"Huh?" I thought the cold must be making her crazy.

"The most important thing is finding Morph and stopping Dr. Demonax from taking his crazy plan any further," Zoe explained. "If we separate, we double our chances of finding Morph quickly. I want to grow up and go to college, not become a slave to robot penguins!"

"A good idea in theory," I agreed through my chattering teeth. "But in case you haven't noticed, we're locked in an underground room and there's only one way out—the ice corridor."

"If I picked this lock, I bet I can pick the lock up there," she said, pointing to the hatch door that Dr. Demonax and his crazed penguins had thrown us down.

"But even if we do open that door," I argued, "I bet it's guarded by penguins. I bet Dr. Demonax is standing there waiting to throw us back down again."

"And I bet Morph is up there!" said Zoe.

I thought about it for a minute. It seemed crazy—so crazy, it might work.

"Fine," I said. "Let's give it a try."

Zoe went to work with her bobby pin, and sure enough, after a few pokes, the basement hatch sprang open.

"Pass me the periscope," Zoe said.

I passed it to her, and slowly she pushed the top mirror up through the hatch. As she looked into the bottom mirror, I watched her do a full 360 with the periscope to check that no one was waiting in the laboratory.

"I don't see anything," she whispered. "The coast is clear."

Quickly, she began to climb out of the hatch.

"Wait!" I whispered, "Take this." Reaching into the bag stuffed with Dr. Demonax's inventions, I pulled out the pair of walkie-talkie earplugs and threw one of them to Zoe. "Keep in touch with me, OK?"

"OK," she smiled as she caught it.

Quietly, Zoe closed the hatch door behind her as she climbed up into the domed laboratory. I turned back to the ice corridor and began to walk toward it. Pushing the other walkie-talkie earplug deep into my ear, I began to walk through the frosty tunnel. At first it was large enough to walk through, but soon it got smaller and smaller and I had to start crawling on the ice.

My jeans got soaked through with icy water and my knees burned with the cold. Soon everything turned numb as I crawled on hands and knees that felt like dead weights.

At the end of the tunnel there was a tiny door, and as I crawled toward it, I prayed that it wasn't locked. Zoe might have been a car thief in the making, but I didn't have a clue how to pick a lock. I crawled up to the door, my body aching from the cold. Sure enough, the door was locked shut, but this time there was no lock to pick— there was a code to crack. A cushion pad sat next to the door with the words:

THE YEAR THE REPUBLIC OF SINGAPORE WAS FOUNDED

There was no way I wanted to risk getting the code wrong, so I touched the earplug in my ear and whispered Zoe's name: "Zoe, Zoe, come in, Zoe."

"Yes, Will," I heard a crackling voice say over the walkie-talkie.

"Where are you?" I asked, my voice trembling with cold.

"In Dr. Demonax's snowmobile garage. No sign of Morph yet," Zoe replied.

It was hurting my throat to speak, I was so cold. "Listen," I croaked, "I need you to help me crack a code."

"I'll try," Zoe said.

I told her the sentence about Singapore. Zoe was bound to know the answer as she'd lived there. She was silent for a while and then she said, "1891."

It took me a stupid amount of time to raise my numb fingers to the keypad and type 1891 into it. I was slowly freezing into a solid boy-shaped block of ice. Amazingly, the door lock released. "Success!" I cried happily.

Zoe whispered into her walkie-talkie, "Let me know what you find."

The door swung open and suddenly my heart froze like an iceberg. In front of me was an icy underground cave. Just like in the lab, a giant black pillar stood in the middle of the room, and running from the pillar were thousands of wires—

each wire had a robotic penguin attached to it. At the top of the pillar were two spinning metal balls that were bouncing off each other like magnets.

That was it! The pillar in the middle of the dome was the power source! The penguins were being recharged on it!

A gigantic TV screen was wedged into the far wall of the cave. On the TV screen were images of important places around the world: the White House, the houses of Parliament, the Taj Mahal, the Eiffel Tower, the Great Barrier Reef. Underneath each picture on the screen was the word "TARGET" in red letters.

There must have been thousands of penguins in the underground chamber. The ones that weren't charging themselves on the large pillar were marching in unison, their heads raised to the TV screen, studying it carefully. I watched in

horror as the image on the screen turned into Dr. Demonax's snot-filled face.

"My super-strength magnet fields are sucking dark energy from the universe to fuel you all," he was saying. "I have created you, my droid army, to take over the world one rotten country at a time. Fueled by dark energy, there will be nothing that can stop you!"

I had to stop him! I had to stop Dr. Demonax from taking over the world. If only I could find a way to destroy the large column of dark energy that was feeding the droid army with power. Without an army, Dr. Demonax could never take over the world. But I couldn't do it alone—my arms and legs were frozen stiff, and there was no way I'd make it over to the dark energy column without being pecked to death by droid penguins.

Crawling backwards into the icy tunnel, I

closed the tiny door behind me. Using my walkie-talkie ear plug, I tried to contact Zoe as quietly as I could: "Zoe, Zoe, come in, Zoe."

"Will?" a voice answered.

"I know how to stop the droids!"

"Will, they're everywhere," she said in panic.

"What?"

"The penguins, they're all around me. They're closing in on me. HELP!"

My aching, freezing limbs scurried back through the icy corridor as quickly as they could. Everything felt as if it was freezing inside of me: my heart, my lungs, my stomach, everything hurt from the cold. But soon I'd managed to pull myself back into the underground room full of inventions. My aching hands could no longer carry the bag full of inventions, so I left it behind as I started to climb the stairs to the hatch door.

"Zoe?" I said through the walkie-talkie. There was no answer.

Pulling myself through the hatch, I made my way back into the laboratory. Quickly, I ran toward the door to the outside world. I forgot to put on my snowsuit and ran outside into the blistering cold in nothing but my soaking jeans and sweater. My teeth knocked against each other like claps of thunder as I tried to run toward the snowmobile garage. There were penguins everywhere, and as they started waddling toward me, their metallic jaws were snapping like a bear trap.

I could hear Zoe screaming—the shrill sound of her voice was carried to me on the subzero wind. My voice froze in my throat as I tried to scream back. I wanted to tell her I was on my way but no words would come out.

I could feel my breathing getting shallow, and my body was shaking so violently that every time I blinked I thought my eyes were going to freeze shut. The garage was in sight—it was only a few steps away, but there were dozens of penguins. They were everywhere I looked. Zoe was standing just inside the garage, being held by the hair by Dr. Demonax. In his other hand Dr. Demonax was holding Morph.

I tried to run toward her, I tried to scream, but all I remember is my freezing body refusing to move. I fell down into the snow, my eyelids closed, and I blacked out.

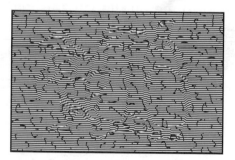

They're everywhere!!!

Hours could have passed while I was unconscious; I have no idea. What I do know is what Zoe told me later—apparently Dr. Demonax dragged me out of the snow and back to his lab. He tied Zoe into a chair, and as she watched, he lay me down on a human-shaped radiator to thaw me out, before tying me to a chair too.

When I woke up I was warm again. My teeth had stopped chattering, my frozen veins had thawed out, and it didn't hurt to breathe anymore. Don't get me wrong, I was relieved to discover I hadn't been stamped to death by a herd of droid penguins, or frozen in a block of ice, or that I was swimming around inside the stomach of an Antarctic whale. But I wasn't that happy to see I was in Dr. Demonax's lab tied up.

My ankles were clamped to the chair. Large leather straps secured my arms to the chair's armrests. I tried to wriggle free, but it was no use. A large leather strap wrapped around my forehead, holding my head to the back of the chair.

Zoe was making a whimpering noise to the left of me, but my head was strapped in so tightly I couldn't turn to look at her.

Now Dr. Demonax was strolling into my line of vision. Two penguins stood beside him, their beady eyes fixed on me and Zoe. I wanted to fight Dr. Demonax and his stupid penguins, but the straps holding me down were too strong and I couldn't budge.

A sick grin spread over Dr. Demonax's face as he watched me struggle.

"You saved me from freezing to death so you could capture me?" I cried at him.

"Until I have Morph working, I need you alive," he said slowly, enjoying each word as if it was a tasty treat.

"Please just let us go. We won't tell anyone you're trying to take over the world with penguins," Zoe sobbed.

"SILENCE, STUPID GIRL!" Dr. Demonax bellowed at Zoe.

At that moment I hated Dr. Demonax more than I hated anyone. It wasn't Zoe's fault that his stupid plan had been foiled—how dare he yell at her!

"I hadn't planned on you being here," he sneered at Zoe. "I was hoping Will would find me one day but I hadn't expected him to bring a little friend with him."

"Just because you're a lonely, snot-slurping freak doesn't mean other people don't have friends," I said.

But this only made Dr. Demonax even angrier. He clenched his fists and raised his shoulders up to his ears, then he began to shout...

"All my life I've had to deal with bullies like you! At school people used to pick on me. 'Hey, snot-face!' they'd yell. Booger brains, snot monster, nose dribbler—I had a string of nasty names. I can't help it if my nose is moist! Then I met Henry Solvit. He was the first person to see the man behind my dripping nose. We helped each other create wonderful inventions, but then he met your mother and they had you."

I tried to break in, but Dr. Demonax cut me off.

Disgusting boogers!

"I was alone again," he went on. "No one would be my friend. I grew to HATE humanity so I moved to the South Pole to get away from everyone. I built my droid penguins for company, but I soon realized they could be so much more. I discovered that by using super-strength magnets, I could suck dark energy out of the universe and use it to fuel a droid army. With the help of my droid army, I would be able to make the world understand how it feels to be me."

"But that's just crazy," I broke in.

"Crazy? Are you calling me crazy?" the mad professor started, his eyes flashing. "Just see how crazy I can be. I will infect everyone who ever lives with my snot virus—soon every person on the planet will suffer as I have suffered!" Dr. Demonax said, wiping his nose on the sleeve of his white lab coat. "I need Morph to transform into a time machine so I can take the penguins back to the beginning of the dawn of humankind—then I can infect them all with my sneezing sickness!"

"Morph will only work for me," I said quietly, knowing that this was a lie, that Morph's time machine doesn't work for anyone; it has a mind of its own. "Give it to me and I'll help you use it."

"Like I'm going to just hand the greatest invention ever created back to a child who has no idea of its power!" Dr. Demonax snorted.

"Fine, if you don't give Morph back to me then you'll never be able to use the time machine—EVER!" I said.

Dr. Demonax looked thoughtful for a moment. It was as if he knew that he had no choice. He hesitated before taking a deep breath and beginning to speak. "Will you promise to stay here with me?" he asked, his eyes widening like a puppy dog's.

"Excuse me?" I nearly fainted with shock.

"I like having you here—it's not so... so... lonely." His mad eyes widened with mania and a huge snot bubble grew out of his right nostril, popping and splattering everywhere.

"You want me to stay here?" I asked, trying not to be sick at the sight of Dr. Demonax and his snot-filled face.

"You could be my assistant!" he grinned madly.

Obviously, I'd rather have an eternally snotty

NO WAY!!

nose than stay in the Antarctic as Dr. Demonax's assistant. I was an Adventurer—I had more important things to do. But a plan was hatching in my head.

"OK," I agreed.

"Will!" Zoe screamed.

"There's no other way," I said, trying to sound as defeated as possible.

Dr. Demonax threw his hands into the air with joy then rushed toward me before leaning over to release the straps tying me to the electric chair. His gross nose was right in my face, and I just tried to focus on my plan.

"Will, HELP!" Zoe begged. I ran over and untied her in no time at all.

"Look," I said. "We need to get back down into that ice tunnel and deactivate the dark energy power source. Once that's done we can get out of here. Before we do anything, we need our snowsuits. No way am I nearly freezing to death twice in one day."

"OK," Zoe agreed as we both ran to put them on.

Hot beneath our snow gear, we headed toward the trap door that led down to the basement. I lifted the heavy hatch door open and climbed down the ladder.

The bag stuffed full of Dr. Demonax's inventions was still sitting on the ground, and I remembered the freeze gun I'd stashed in the bag. I pulled it out.

"Take this," I told Zoe as she climbed down into the basement.

The door to the ice tunnel had been left open. A frosty breeze chilled my face as I pulled the hood of the snowsuit around my head so the only things exposed to the cold were my eyes.

"Ready to save the world?" I said to Zoe.

"You bet!" She nodded and took a deep breath as we both walked through the door into the ice tunnel.

Scrambling through the ice tunnel was easy with my snowsuit on. Zoe and I reached the end in no time at all.

"So this is where Dr. Demonax has been training his droid army?" Zoe asked, looking at the door that led to the underground cave.

"Yup, this is it," I nodded.

"So do we have a plan?" she asked. "How are we going to get through the army of killer penguins to deactivate the giant magnets?"

"We'll need to fight our way through," I told her. "I'll use Morph, you use the freeze gun. Together we should be able to hold off the droids long enough to destroy their power supply."

I tapped "1891" into the keypad on the wall, and the small door creaked open. The scene inside the cave was exactly as I remembered it: thousands of droid penguins marching, training for battle, and charging themselves on the pillar of dark energy.

Slowly, I crawled through the door, out into the underground cave. Zoe stayed close behind me. "When I count to three, let it rip with your freeze gun," I called over my shoulder. "Shoot any droid in sight and I'll do the same.

Then we need to run towards the column. When we're there, you hold the droids off and I'll get to work destroying Dr. Demonax's power source."

I took a deep breath and prepared myself for battle. "One... Two... Three..."

The sound of power blasting through the air consumed the cave. Soon every droid penguin in the room had seen me and Zoe and they were heading toward us.

I aimed my stun gun at the nearest one and shot it between the eyes. It began to shake and rattle from side to side; smoke poured out of its nose and ears as it short-circuited and fell to the icy ground.

As I blasted my way through the droid-packed cave, from the corner of my eye I saw Zoe freezing every penguin in sight. When she fired her freeze gun a blast of liquid nitrogen flew

KAPOWWoW!!

BOOM!!

through the air and splattered over the droids, solidifying on impact and freezing them rigid.

"Nice work!" I shouted, impressed by how well she was doing.

As thousands of robotic penguins waddled toward us with menace in their eyes, Zoe and I stood back to back and blasted them, and slowly moved toward the whirring magnetic column. Soon there were thousands of stunned and frozen droids around us—so many that we had to climb over them as we walked.

Eventually we worked our way to the heart of the room. The pillar stretched from floor to ceiling and buzzed with the power of the magnetic field that flowed through it. The two large magnets at the top of the pillar spun and circled each other as they worked to suck mysterious dark energy from the universe.

"Remember the plan, Zoe," I yelled at her. "You hold off the droids, I'll find a way to destroy the power source."

Quickly, I ran through Morph's programs in my head, trying to think of the best thing I could use to destroy a magnetic power cell of dark energy. Submarine, time machine, spaceship, skate ramp, racing car—nothing seemed suitable. Then it struck me—the stun gun in my hand was my best bet. I could shoot at the magnets, and if it smashed the pillar around them, it might stop them from working. There was a chance it wouldn't work, but there was a chance that it would—and that was the only chance I had.

"I can't hold them off much longer, Will," Zoe shouted. "There are too many of them."

Without a second thought, I aimed and pulled the trigger faster than an Olympic sprinter. Morph spun violently in my hands and started to spark with neon lights. The glass pillar cracked and shattered around me and as I lifted my hands above my head to protect myself from the falling shards of glass, the spinning magnets inside the pillar began to glow like a ball of pure white energy. Nervously, I held the stun gun toward the magnets again and shot them once more.

The sound of heavy machinery grinding to a halt nearly deafened me. What was left of the glass pillar began to shake as a scorching blue light rippled from the base of the generator to the cave roof. Soon the whole column was glowing like a neon flame.

My eyes squinted shut as I tried to hold the stun gun in place. If only I could keep shooting, it would destroy the dark energy source for good.

A sound like a volcanic eruption blasted

Volcano —————→

around me. I heard Zoe scream. Then everything went eerily silent.

Slowly, I pried my eyes open and looked around. The pillar has smashed into millions of pieces. Broken glass lay all around me. My hands were shaking, but I managed to deactivate Morph and put the tiny stun gun into my pocket.

Turning around, I could see thousands of robotic penguins frozen and stunned still. Now that their power source had been destroyed, they'd never move again.

Then I saw Zoe. She'd turned as pale as a ghost and looked as if she wanted to cry.

"We've done it, Will," she whispered to me. "We've saved the world."

Woohoo!

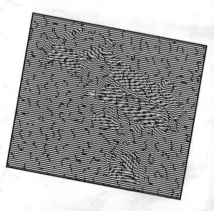

Zoe was right, we had saved the world. But we still needed to get out of Antarctica and away from Dr. Demonax. Quickly we climbed over the thousands of deactivated droids in the cave, back through the ice tunnel, and into the tiny basement. As I picked up the heavy bag with Dr. Demonax's inventions in it, we made our way toward the ladder.

"Use this," Zoe said, handing me the periscope. I checked that the coast was clear before climbing into the laboratory and let out a gasp. There was no sign of Dr. Demonax—not at all—his body wasn't where we had left it after I'd

Uh-oh!

stunned him with Morph. He'd disappeared.

"Let's get out of here fast," I said.

Quickly we collected all of our things (including Dr Demonax's suit that goes through glass – that thing is awesome) and headed toward the door to the outside world. A blizzard stormed into us as we pushed back the door.

"We need to get to the ocean!" I shouted. "Once we're there, we can activate Morph into a boat or submarine—anything that will take us home."

I pulled my compass that always points home out of my bag. "This way!" I shouted, pointing in the direction of the compass's needle.

We'd only taken a few steps when we heard the clank of metal storm towards us. One glance back toward the domed laboratory and my worst nightmares were confirmed. There were more droids, and they were heading right for us.

Zoe and I ran through the snow with the killer droid penguins on our tail, hearing the clank of their metal jaws and the thud of their heavy feet behind us.

"I thought we'd deactivated them all when we shut off their power source," Zoe screamed.

"Maybe some of them still have some juice left," I guessed as I leapt over a snow bank, running as fast as my legs would take me.

Glancing down I typed the word "snowmobile" into Morph. Then, quickly, I threw Morph to the ground. As Morph hit the floor, it sprang back up, transforming into a snowmobile in the air. It hit the ground speeding, and Zoe and I jumped on as it zoomed over the snow. Throwing our bags into the back of the snowmobile, I put my foot down on the accelerator.

The snowmobile flew over a cliff, plummeted down, and turned into a boat as it hit the water.

I thought we were safe, but I was wrong. Dr. Demonax stood on the top of the cliff, watching as the penguins threw themselves over the side one by one.

"You'll never stop me!" he cried.

The penguins started to swim toward us at the speed of a hungry shark so we led them further out to sea.

Before we knew it, Dr. Demonax appeared on a speedboat, chasing us through the icy waters.

"Reach into the bag and pull out anything we can shoot at him with!" I cried as Zoe scrambled in the bag and pulled a giant freeze gun out.

Quick as a flash, she pointed the gun at the penguins swimming near us, fired, and soon they were frozen solid.

But the freeze gun wouldn't work for long, we were moving too quickly—it was impossible for Zoe to get a good aim. Nothing would stop Dr. Demonax and his droid penguins.

"Can we turn Morph into a submarine?" Zoe shouted.

"I can't risk turning Morph like that and not being inside—one toe in that water and we'll freeze to death!" I threw my head to the sky in despair, desperate for some kind of clue to know how to escape. Something was moving between the clouds, it wasn't a plane... it was a helicopter!

"Zoe, look!" I shouted, pointing up to the sky.

But my voice was drowned out by the sound of the helicopter chopping down through the sky toward us. The side door opened and I braced myself for penguins to start falling out of the sky.

But miraculously, there weren't any black and white creatures appearing. Instead, I saw Stanley poking his face out the side of the helicopter before throwing two ropes down into the sea.

Dr. Demonax's boat pulled up alongside Morph, but, just as he started saying something to me, the sound of the helicopter drowned him out. I steered Morph towards the ropes dangling down from the helicopter as Dr. Demonax followed closely behind. Penguins were swimming around us everywhere I looked, we were inches away from the ladder—I had no idea how I was meant to climb it without losing Zoe, Morph, and the bag of inventions sitting in the back of the boat.

Now Zoe was shouting at me but I just couldn't hear her. I steered Morph till we were just below the helicopter's dangling ropes, and Zoe jumped up into the air, caught one of the ropes, pulled it down and fastened it to the side of the boat.

I swung the boat around so Zoe could reach the other rope and she threw me the freeze gun. I started blasting the droids that were swimming toward us.

I felt the boat begin to rock and sway before lifting off into the air. Glancing above me, I saw Stanley and another man winch us up to the helicopter. Dr. Demonax stood up in his boat, clenched his fists, and started to yell into the air. The sound of his words was drowned out by the helicopter's rotor blades and as we flew high into the sky, I watched him getting smaller and smaller...

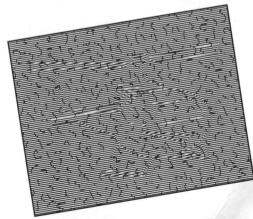

CHAPTER ELEVEN
BACK HOME

The next 24 hours of my life passed in a bit of a blur. Stanley's helicopter took us to South America, then we flew the rest of the way home in a regular airplane.

One of the helicopter pilots told me that the secret service had been spying on Dr. Demonax for years. They said I was a better spy than any of them were because I'd been able to work undercover to foil Dr. Demonax's plans. On the plane back home, I thought about spying on Dr. Demonax and wondered if spying was going to be my special Adventuring skill, just like Grandpa. But I knew deep down that spying wasn't my special skill, it was something else—I

When would I find out what u special skill is?

just hadn't figured it out yet.

When the airplane touched down, Zoe's mom was there to meet her. I don't think she was mad at Zoe for running away, she just seemed really pleased to see her. No one was there to meet me though, and Stanley drove me back to Solvit Hall without saying a single word.

I opened the door to Solvit Hall and expected Plato to come running toward me, but he didn't. Grandpa was nowhere to be seen, so I trudged up the stairs and headed for my room.

Grandpa Monty was sitting on the edge of my bed as I walked into the room. Plato was lying at his feet, but soon stood up and wagged his tail when he saw me.

"You OK, Grandpa?" I asked, afraid that I'd really upset him by running away. "Bet you didn't even notice I was gone?" I joked.

Grandpa looked up at me with his pale eyes. "The house has been quiet without you."

"Well, it's a good job I managed to fight off Dr. Demonax's droid army and come home safely, isn't it?" I smiled, patting Plato on the head.

"Get some sleep," Grandpa said, leaning on his walking stick and standing up. "But first, turn the TV on and watch the news."

Grandpa walked out of my bedroom and closed the door behind him, leaving me and Plato alone. Plato licked my face and barked with happiness as I gave him a quick wrestle.

I pulled Morph out of my pocket, turned it into a TV and switched channels until I found the news.

There was a newsreader sitting behind a desk. This is what she said, "Last night over one hundred robotic penguins were found frozen in the Antarctic Ocean. They belonged to the elusive Dr. Demonax, the gifted inventor who has lived in Antarctica for many years. After years of solitude, Dr. Demonax has gone mad and has been taken into police custody for his own safety."

So that was it, the last of the droid penguins had frozen in the sea and Dr. Demonax was finally behind bars. Another Adventure had come to an end. There was just one more thing I needed to do.

I activated Morph, stood back and watched as it turned into a time machine. I had no way to control where Morph took me in time, but the time machine always seemed to take me to where I needed to go. With any luck, just this once, where I needed to go and where I wanted to go would be the same place.

It only took a few seconds of whizzing through

time before Morph stopped traveling and landed down in the alleyway I'd found myself in before, the time I traveled into the future and met Mikey.

Climbing out of the time machine, I deactivated Morph and put it in my pocket. Unlike last time, the alleyway was clean, there was no rubbish on the ground. I walked towards the end of the alleyway, onto a busy street full of cars and people. Instantly I knew that this wasn't the same future I'd traveled to before.

There wasn't that much about the place that was different from modern day, people were wearing weird clothes but other than that, technology didn't seem to have advanced much in a few years. That's when I promised myself that one time I was going to travel into the distant future—how amazing would it be to see what kind of gadgets and gizmos people have in 100's of years time?

As I walked through the bustling streets, something in the corner of my vision caught my attention. Strolling down the street, with a toy T-rex in his hand was Mikey. Only he didn't look like he did before, his face was clean, and his clothes weren't torn and tattered. He was holding a woman's hand, I guessed that was his mom, and she was walking arm in hand with Mikey's dad.

Right then and there, walking down the street in the future, I realized for the first time just how important it is to be an Adventurer. If it hadn't been for me, Mikey, his parents, and every other person alive would be dribbling with boogers and working as slaves to Dr. Demonax right now.

Happy that the future was safe from droids, I strolled back to the alleyway to activate Morph and go home. But there was one piece of rubbish sitting in the alleyway now. As I got closer, I realized it wasn't rubbish at all. It was another letter, a letter with my name on it.

Congratulations, Will.

You've not only completed another Adventure but you've realized how important it is for you to follow your destiny.

Your next Adventure will take you back in time again, to a place where you will learn about your parents.

Here's a clue to where you'll be going next:
The tigers there are slightly unusual.

As ever, I had no idea what the clue in the letter meant and no idea where I was going next. But one thing I did know is that the next Adventure definitely had something to do with Mom and Dad—finally I was getting closer to discovering the truth about what happened to them.

I activated Morph and it spun wildly before popping up into a time machine. I climbed in and waited for it to take me home. I couldn't wait to get back to Solvit Hall, play with Plato and hang out with Grandpa—I even hoped he'd cooked something crazy for tea!

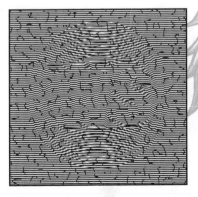